the BEST NEWS ever

STORY BY: BECKY olmstead

PICTURES BY: NINA heintz

"

You hold in your hands a very precious and important book. I do not know of a more passionate and credible advocate for children than my friend Becky Olmstead. *The Best News Ever* is a great resource for anyone working with kids, or a parent wanting to share Jesus with their child in a fresh, simple way.

WESS STAFFORD
President Emeritus,
Compassion International

This book is dedicated to
every child everywhere.

May you know...

That you were created with a purpose and a plan,
to dream big dreams, see impossible things,
and change the world with the power
and love that lives inside you.

you are loved.

From the beginning
GOD WANTED A WORLD
filled with KIDS!
All throughout history
GOD HAS SEEN KIDS AS
SPECIAL

and this is the ...

BEST
NEWS
EVER!

and this is what

HE LOVES

about them...

GOD LOVES THAT KIDS BRING

JOY

In the Bible, the book God gave us, there was a super old woman NAMED SARAH who was sad that she didn't have any children. God gave her a baby.

SHE LAUGHED WITH JOY because she was so happy!

WANT TO KNOW WHAT ELSE GOD LOVES?

A LITTLE BOY NAMED SAMUEL heard someone call his name one night as he lay in bed.

AT FIRST HE DIDN'T RECOGNIZE THE VOICE, but then he learned that GOD WAS CALLING HIM.

God wanted to tell Samuel an important message.

WANT TO KNOW WHAT ELSE GOD LOVES?

GOD LOVES THAT KIDS CAN BE

BRAVE

a young girl named Miriam
had a big job to do.
HER MOTHER SENT HER
to watch over her baby brother when
HE WAS IN A DANGEROUS RIVER
and she kept him safe.

WANT TO KNOW WHAT ELSE
GOD LOVES?

GOD LOVES THAT KIDS CAN GIVE

WHEN PEOPLE WERE HUNGRY, a small boy was willing to share his lunch with Jesus.

HE GOT TO BE PART OF A

MIRACLE

that Jesus did to feed lots of people with what *he gave.*

WANT TO KNOW WHAT ELSE GOD LOVES?

Jesus told His friends,
"LET THE LITTLE CHILDREN
COME TO ME,
DON'T STOP THEM!"

He wanted kids to know that
they were always welcome
to come and be close to Him.

WANT TO KNOW WHAT ELSE GOD LOVES?

GOD LOVES YOU!

YOU WERE HIS DREAM.

HE BROUGHT YOU INTO THE WORLD for a purpose.

and He made you **uniquely** you.

HE LIKES YOU JUST THE WAY YOU ARE He has given you special talents and abilities so you can use them to bring His love to others.

GOD KNOWS ALL THE GOOD THINGS THAT ARE IN YOU. But, He also knows that you aren't perfect. He knows that you sometimes do wrong things and that you may have had wrong things done to you.

THOSE DARK THOUGHTS, FEELINGS OR ACTIONS

that sometimes rise up
inside you, can hurt
other people and keep you
from knowing and
experiencing God's love.

BUT GOD HAS WAY
BETTER THINGS FOR YOU!

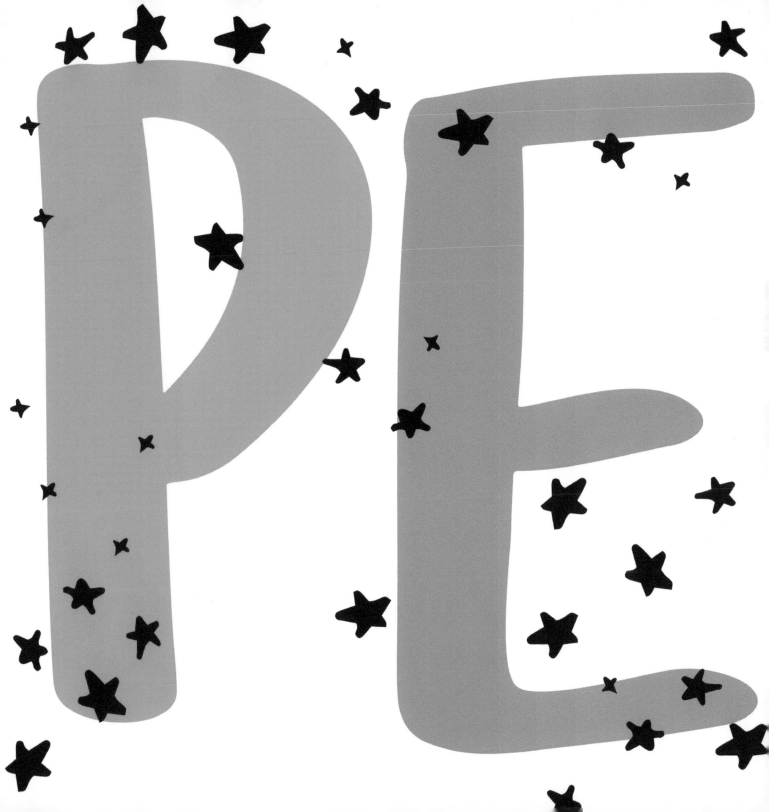

He loves you so much that He sent His Son, Jesus, to earth.

Someone had to pay for all the wrong things we've done.

Jesus chose to pay that price when He died on a cross.

THREE DAYS LATER,

God brought Him back to life so that nothing can ever separate you, or anyone else, from experiencing

GOD'S LOVE!

It's like a great, big gift God wants to give you.

WHEN YOU SAY, "YES"

God puts His Holy Spirit inside of you

The Holy Spirit

CHANGES
YOUR HEART

so that you can love
God and love others.

THIS GOOD NEWS IS FOR ALL KIDS, EVERYWHERE.

It doesn't matter who you are or where you live or what you've done. **GOD WANTS ALL KIDS** to come to Him and say, "YES."

If you want to say "YES" to receiving this gift of love, you can pray this prayer.

Prayer is talking to God just like you would TALK TO YOUR BEST FRIEND.

Hi God,

I want to say "Yes" to you. Thank you for loving me and for sending Jesus to pay the price for all the wrong things I do. I welcome Your powerful Holy Spirit into my life. Thank you that You promise to always be with me. You want to be close to me, and that You want to talk to me. Is there anything You want to say to me right now?

(WAIT QUIETLY FOR A MINUTE TO LISTEN.)

Goodbye God.

IF YOU PRAYED THIS PRAYER, TELL SOMEONE.

Always remember that today you said,

"YES"

to receiving God's gift of love!

check it

GENESIS 1:28

GENESIS 21:1-7

1 SAMUEL 3:1-19

EXODUS 2:1-10

JOHN 6:9-13

LUKE 18:16

PSALM 139:13-16

GENESIS 8:21

out!

THE BEST NEWS EVER—IT'S ALL IN THE BIBLE!

HOPE   **1 JOHN 4:9-10**

     1 JOHN 4:13

     HEBREWS 13:5

     JOHN 3:16

BECKY OLMSTEAD | FORT COLLINS, COLORADO

ABOUT THE AUTHOR

Becky Olmstead has been influential in putting words to a God-dream for the next generation, and has given her life to the cause of making Jesus known on the earth. Her heart beats for seeing a generation of kids ignited with the love and power of God like never before.

NINA HEINTZ | SAN LUIS OBISPO, CALIFORNIA

ABOUT THE ILLUSTRATOR

Ever since she has been a kid, Nina Heintz has experienced God's love and power as she expresses herself creatively. As a graphic designer she gets to create with beauty and share the gospel message through art.